SICKLE CELL ANEMIA

SICKLE CELL ANEMIA

Ruth Bjorklund

 **Marshall Cavendish**
Benchmark
New York

Special thanks to Shayla Bergmann, MD, Medical University of South Carolina, department of pediatric hematology/oncology, for her expert review of the manuscript.

Other Marshall Cavendish Offices:
Marshall Cavendish International (Asia) Private Limited, 1 New Industrial Road, Singapore 536196 • Marshall Cavendish International (Thailand) Co Ltd. 253 Asoke, 12th Flr, Sukhumvit 21 Road, Klongtoey Nua, Wattana, Bangkok 10110, Thailand • Marshall Cavendish (Malaysia) Sdn Bhd, Times Subang, Lot 46, Subang Hi-Tech Industrial Park, Batu Tiga, 40000 Shah Alam, Selangor Darul Ehsan, Malaysia

Marshall Cavendish is a trademark of Times Publishing Limited

All websites were available and accurate when this book was sent to press.

Library of Congress Cataloging-in-Publication Data

Bjorklund, Ruth.
Sickle cell anemia / by Ruth Bjorklund.
p. cm. — (Health alert)
Summary: "Provides comprehensive information on the causes, treatment, and history of sickle cell anemia"—Provided by publisher.
Includes index.
ISBN 978-0-7614-4821-1
1. Sickle cell anemia—Juvenile literature. 2. Genetic disorders—Juvenile literature. I. Title.
RC641.7.S5B556 2011
616.1′527—dc22
2009051254

Front cover: Red blood cells, both normal and sickle-shaped, as seen under a microscope.
Title page: Red blood cells flowing through a vein.

Editor: Joy Bean
Publisher: Michelle Bisson
Art Director: Anahid Hamparian

Photo research by Candlepants Incorporated
Cover Photo: Eye of Science / Photo Researchers Inc.

The photographs in this book are used by permission and through the courtesy of:
Alamy Images: Fabian Schmidt, 1; Corbis Premium, 10; Phototake Inc, 15; MedicalRF.com, 19, 43; Sebastian Kaulitzki, 45; Image Source, 47; Bubbles Photolibrary, 51. *Getty Images*: Dr. Stanley Flegler, 5, 17, 26; AE Pictures Inc., 7; 3D4Medical.com, 21; DK Stock/ Jaimie D Travis, 25; Geoff du Feu, 31; Steve Dunwell, 35; Darren Hauck, 38; Vince Bucci, 37. *Photo Researchers Inc.*: BSIP, 13; Mauro Fermariello, 41. *AP Images*: 32.

Printed in Malaysia (T)
1 3 5 6 4 2

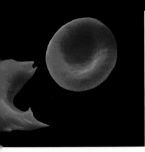

CONTENTS

DEVON'S STORY

Devon lives in a small town. He has a few family friends, but he does not have many neighborhood pals. His best friend, Robi, once lived nearby. Sometimes Robi would ride the school bus home with Devon so that they could do homework or play video games together. On weekends and school breaks, though, it was harder for the boys to see each other. Robi shared a bicycle with his younger brother, so he could not always ride to Devon's house. Devon did not have a bicycle at all, because riding a bike made him feel really tired, and his legs would hurt horribly.

Devon has **sickle cell disease.** The disease has changed some of his **red blood cells.** Red blood cells carry oxygen throughout the body. Normal red blood cells are round, but Devon's are curved into a C shape, or sickle shape, named after a farm tool called a sickle. Devon's abnormal red blood cells have difficulty passing through his blood vessels, so they do not deliver enough oxygen to the other cells in his body. When Devon is **dehydrated**, exhausted, or sick with a cold or flu, he becomes especially low on oxygen. This causes a **pain crisis**—an episode of severe pain.

Last year, Devon experienced more pain than usual. He became very stressed, and that seemed to trigger more severe

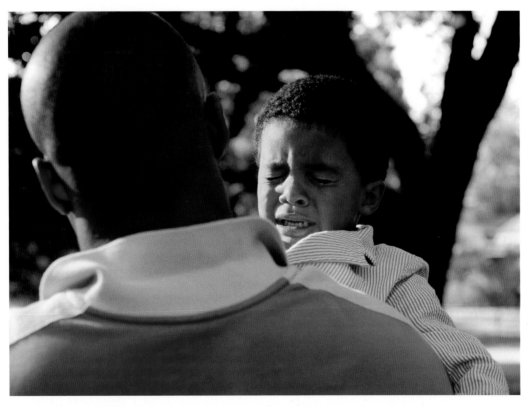

A pain crisis can cause a lot of pain for children with sickle cell anemia, but there are ways to deal with the pain.

and more frequent crises. His friend Robi moved across the country, and Devon felt depressed and lonely. Devon is smaller than most of his classmates and has always been a little shy. It is hard for him to make new friends. A lot of the other boys at school play sports such as soccer and basketball, but Devon can not keep up with the children who play those sports. He can do some activities, such as bowling or swimming, but whenever he feels tired, he has to stop and rest.

Devon wishes he had a brother or sister, but his parents chose not to have any more children once they learned about Devon's sickle cell disease. The disease is inherited, which means that parents pass it on to their children. Neither of Devon's parents has sickle cell disease, but they both have an abnormal **gene** that carries the risk of the disease. Devon was born with sickle cell disease because both of his parents passed along this abnormal gene.

Devon had his first pain crisis when he was six months old. Soon afterward, his doctors ran some tests and discovered Devon's sickle cell disease. One of his doctors prescribed **penicillin** for Devon to take every day. Penicillin is an **antibiotic**, a medicine that fights bacterial infection. Most people take penicillin or a similar medicine after they get a serious bacterial infection. But Devon's immune system had a hard time fighting off germs, so he took penicillin to avoid getting sick in the first place. The germs that cause colds and other mild sicknesses can develop into life-threatening illnesses for young people with sickle cell disease.

When Devon was seven, his doctors said he did not have to take penicillin anymore. They thought his body was strong enough to fight common infections. But Devon still needed to be careful. He had to have a flu shot every winter. When he had pain crises, he took acetaminophen (the active ingredient in the pain reliever Tylenol) to ease his discomfort. If he played too hard or if he stayed outside too long in the winter, his body would ache and his feet would swell. Damaged by the sickle cells, Devon's kidneys did not retain enough fluids. To stay hydrated, he had to drink lots of water.

Despite his efforts to stay healthy, one year Devon caught a cold. It did not go away on its own, and he developed a pounding pain in his chest. Now Devon had **pneumonia**, a serious lung infection that requires strong antibiotics and pain medicine. He went to the hospital and stayed for six days. Doctors gave him an IV, which is a small tube that delivers medicine directly into the bloodstream through a vein. Devon and his parents were frightened that a simple cold could have such dramatic consequences.

Devon was determined not to get sick like that again. He promised to follow his doctors' advice. It was hard for him to accept that he was not as energetic as other kids. He enjoyed being with his friend Robi so much because they could do

People with sickle cell anemia can play sports, but they may have to take more breaks than others and may not be able to play as long as others.

less energetic activities such as watching movies, listening to music, and playing video games. That is why Devon was so miserable when Robi moved so far away. When Robi asked Devon to fly out and visit him in Colorado during summer vacation, Devon was eager to go, but his parents said no. They explained that Devon's body would not get enough oxygen in Colorado, where the air is lower in oxygen due to high elevation. Devon would probably suffer severe pain, and his trip would be ruined. But Devon really wanted to visit his friend. At his next doctor's appointment, Devon asked his doctor if he could go. She said that people with sickle cell disease should avoid high altitudes. For instance, they should not climb mountains or ride in small planes that do not pump in pressurized oxygen. But his doctor had an idea. "Why don't we see if your parents would be willing to drive you to Colorado?" she said. "If you drive, you can stop every day or two and get used to the altitude gradually. You will have to drink a lot of water and listen to your body. If your legs start to throb or if your hands or feet swell, you will have to slow down. But I think you can do it. And if your parents are willing, I know you are strong enough to give it your all."

"I'm going to mail you a postcard from Pikes Peak this summer!" replied Devon.

2

WHAT IS SICKLE CELL ANEMIA?

Sickle cell disease is a serious disease of the blood. There are a few types of sickle cell disease. The most common type is called sickle cell **anemia**. Anemia is a condition in which a person's blood does not contain enough red blood cells. Sickle cell disease prevents the normal flow of oxygen to the body. The abnormal sickle cells are destroyed faster than normal-shaped red blood cells, and this causes anemia.

WHO HAS SICKLE CELL ANEMIA?

Sickle cell anemia is not **contagious**. It is genetic, meaning that a person is born with the disease. Genes are tiny biological units found in every living cell. They determine what the cell will look like and how it will function. Genes pass characteristics, such as height and hair color, from parents to children. Sickle cell anemia is caused by an abnormal gene

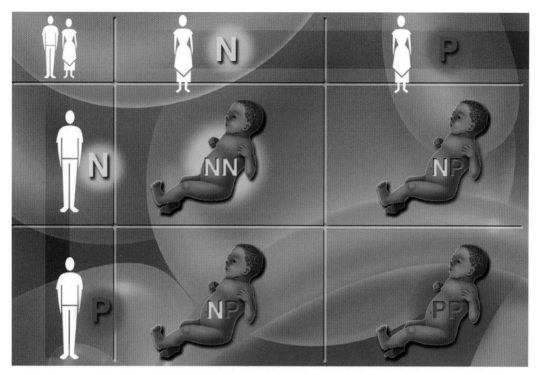

This chart shows the genetic risks of getting sickle cell anemia. If both parents pass on an abnormal "P" gene, the child has a large change of getting the disease. If only one parent passes on an abnormal "P" gene, the child will be healthy but can pass on the gene to his or her children.

that alters the shape of red blood cells. Researchers estimate that more than 2 million Americans carry the sickle cell gene in their bodies. A person carrying just one abnormal sickle cell gene is said to have **sickle cell trait**. People who inherit sickle cell trait never get the disease. However, if two people with sickle cell trait have children together, they could pass the disease to their children.

Because sickle cell anemia is an **inherited** disease, it occurs in groups of people who are closely related. The disease is found in millions of people all over the world, but it is especially common in families whose ancestors come from Africa, South or Central America, India, Saudi Arabia, the Caribbean islands, and Mediterranean countries such as Turkey, Greece, and Italy. Approximately 72,000 Americans have sickle cell disease. The National Institutes of Health (NIH) reports that sickle cell anemia occurs in 1 in 500 African-American births and 1 in 36,000 Latino-American births in the United States.

BLOOD AND THE CIRCULATORY SYSTEM

In order to understand sickle cell anemia, you must first understand more about the blood in your body. The human circulatory system supplies oxygen and nutrients to all the body's cells. Blood vessels are hollow tubes that carry blood to and from the heart. There are three types of blood vessels. Arteries, the largest blood vessels, carry blood away from the heart. Veins carry blood to the heart. **Capillaries**, the smallest vessels, connect arteries and veins.

Oxygen-rich blood travels from the body's main artery, the aorta, throughout the body via other arteries. On the way back to the heart, the blood travels through veins in the lungs, where carbon dioxide is removed from the blood and replaced with oxygen.

To circulate the blood to all parts of the body and back again, the heart must pump with great force. In order to

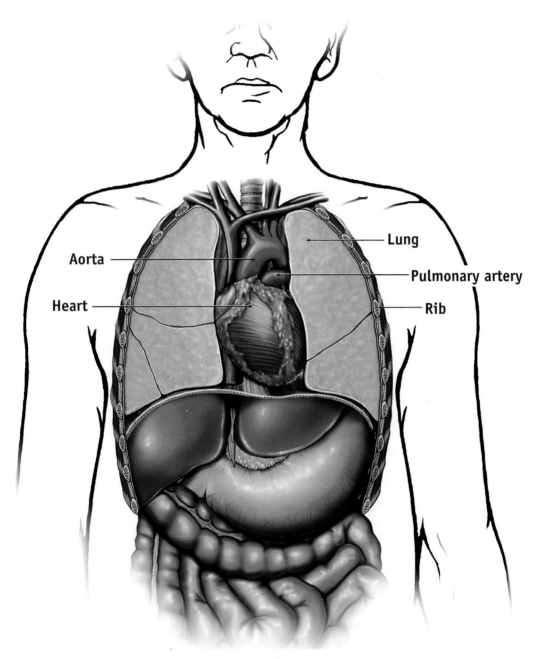

Aorta

Heart

Lung

Pulmonary artery

Rib

The heart is responsible for pumping the blood to all parts of the body.

withstand this force, called blood pressure, arteries must be thick, strong, and very flexible. Every major artery except the pulmonary artery—which supplies blood to the heart itself—branches off from the aorta. These arteries split into medium-sized arteries, which branch off into smaller arteries called arterioles. Arterioles control the blood flowing into the smallest vessels, the capillaries.

Capillaries fan out into a network called a capillary bed. In the capillaries, blood flows along a narrow path, often one blood cell at a time. In the capillary bed, oxygen and nutrients are passed on to the cells, and the blood picks up cell waste. Once it gets filled with carbon dioxide and other cell waste, the blood travels back toward the heart, first through tiny vessels called **venules**. Venules carry the blood to the small veins that are connected to medium and large veins.

BLOOD AT WORK

Blood consists of four main ingredients: red blood cells, white blood cells, platelets, and plasma. Red blood cells, white blood cells, and platelets are solids that the body produces inside bone marrow, the soft tissue inside the large and flat bones of the body. These blood cells are suspended in a liquid called plasma. Whole blood is 55 percent plasma. Red blood cells account for another 40 to 45 percent, and a combination of white blood cells and platelets makes up less than 1 percent.

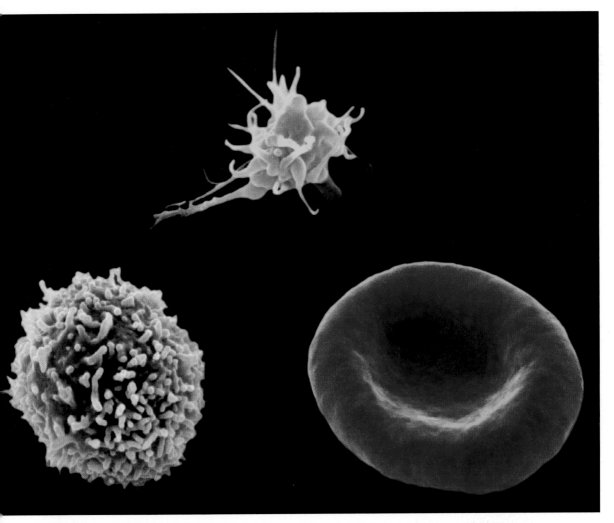

Some of the ingredients that make up blood: (bottom left) white blood cell, (top) platelet, and red blood cell.

An adult human body has about 5 liters (5.3 quarts) of blood flowing through its arteries and veins.

Each type of blood cell has a distinct role in nourishing the body and keeping it healthy. Platelets are responsible for helping blood to clot. Whenever a blood vessel or area of skin is cut, platelets quickly gather at the wound and form a gummy substance to block the flow of blood. On the surface of the skin, this formation is called a scab. White blood cells defend the body against infection.

Plasma is a sticky, yellow-colored fluid that contains water, sugar, salt, hormones (chemical messengers in the body that control organ function), proteins, and minerals. It carries the other blood cells through the body. After delivering oxygen and nourishment, plasma carries the cell waste and debris and passes them through the kidneys, the liver, and the spleen. These organs are responsible for filtering wastes from the bloodstream. Kidneys remove waste from the blood (the body eventually expels this waste through urine). The filtered blood then moves into the liver. Liver cells make proteins from the blood and store the proteins to be used again. The spleen removes germs, dead cells, and abnormally shaped cells from the blood.

RED BLOOD CELLS

Red blood cells, also called RBCs or **erythrocytes**, carry oxygen throughout the body and return with the waste gas carbon dioxide, which we let out when we exhale. In a healthy adult, 2 million RBCs are formed in the bone marrow every second. Each RBC lives for about four months. RBCs are soft, flat, and slightly curved. They easily bend and fold to fit inside the tiny capillary walls.

HEMOGLOBIN

At the center of each red blood cell is a protein molecule called **hemoglobin**. It is made up of two smaller proteins that bind together and carry oxygen and other gases through the body. The two proteins in hemoglobin are called **alpha-globulin** and **beta-globulin**. In normal hemoglobin, the amounts of these

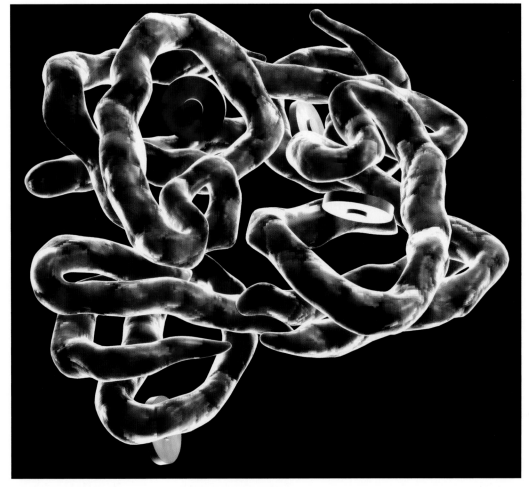

A look at hemoglobin, as seen under a microscope.

two proteins are equal. A third type of protein is called **gamma-globulin**. Gamma-globulin takes the place of beta-globulin in a fetus, but once the baby is born, beta-globulin forms and binds with alpha-globulin, and the gamma-globulin usually disappears.

Hemoglobin in the red blood cells picks up oxygen and transports it to all the muscles, tissues, bones, and organs in the body. Once the hemoglobin has released the oxygen into other cells, it takes away carbon dioxide, a by-product of cell respiration. Cell respiration is the process by which living cells take in oxygen and give off waste such as carbon dioxide. Hemoglobin contains iron, which binds to the oxygen and makes the blood red. When the hemoglobin carries away carbon dioxide, the blood becomes a darker, bluish red.

There are several types of hemoglobin. Hemoglobin A (abbreviated as HbA, Adult Hgb) is the most common and abundant type. About 95 to 98 percent of adults have this type of hemoglobin. Another common type is called hemoglobin A2 (HbA2), which makes up about 2 to 3 percent of red cell hemoglobin in adults. Hemoglobin F (HbF) is found in fetuses and newborns. Our genes determine the type of hemoglobin that our bodies have.

BONE MARROW

Red blood cells, white blood cells, platelets, and hemoglobin are created in bone marrow. Infants have marrow in all their

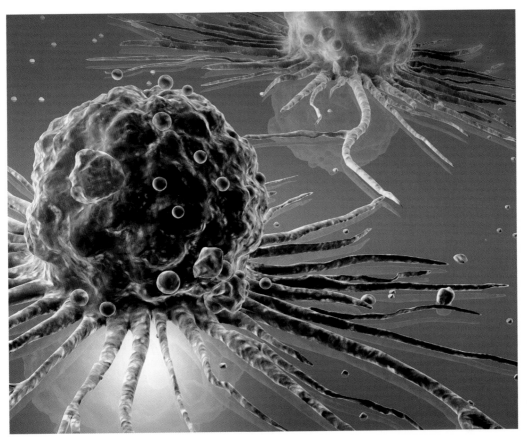

A microscopic view of stem cells.

bones, but in older children and adults, bone marrow is located only in the large, flat bones of the body—such as the hip bone, breast bone, ribs, vertebrae, and shoulder blades—and at the ends of very long bones such as the femur (thigh bone). There are two types of bone marrow: yellow and red. Yellow marrow contains many more fat cells than red marrow. Some white blood cells are made in yellow marrow. Red marrow is a spongy tissue made up of blood vessels, **stem cells**, and proteins. Stem cells are immature cells whose **daughter cells** can develop into any type of cell. When blood cells die or become damaged, weakened, or unhealthy, the stem cells in the bone marrow make replacement blood cells.

SICKLE CELL ANEMIA

People with sickle cell disease do not have normal hemoglobin (HbA or HbA2). Their alpha-globulin protein is normal, but the genes in their beta-globulin are mutated, or changed. This mutation causes the red blood cells to take on a curved C shape. The abnormal RBCs become stiff and thick, and they stick together. Sickle cells clog the bloodstream, especially in the narrowest blood vessels—the capillaries and the venules— and prevent blood from reaching all areas of the body.

When most of a person's RBCs are sickle cells, the body's tissues are deprived of oxygen. This causes severe pain, dangerous infections, and organ damage. It also disturbs the normal chemical balance of the body's cells. Calcium and potassium are minerals that are necessary to keep water flowing in and out of cells. Sickle cells interfere with this process and leave the cells dehydrated. The more dehydrated the body becomes, the more sickle cells are created and the stickier they become. It becomes a cycle of cell damage and pain. Normal red blood cells release a gas called nitric oxide, which keeps blood vessels relaxed and flexible. Sickle cells do not release nitric oxide. Sickle cells live for 10 to 20 days, while normal RBCs live for 90 to 120 days. Sickle cells die so fast that the body cannot make enough RBCs to keep up. This leads to anemia.

SYMPTOMS OF SICKLE CELL DISEASE

The symptoms of sickle cell disease vary, depending on the person, from mild to severe. People with sickle cell trait have few or no symptoms. Some people with sickle cell anemia feel healthy most of the time, while others are frequently hospitalized. The most common symptoms of sickle cell disease are exhaustion, shortness of breath, pale skin, yellowed eyes (a condition called **jaundice**), and weakness due to the reduced amount of oxygen the body receives. Many people experience vision problems because sickle cells block the tiny vessels in their eyes.

People with sickle cell disease are prone to serious infections because their spleens are damaged. When sickle cells block vessels in the spleen, infections rapidly become hard to control, especially for children. Particularly dangerous conditions include **meningitis**, an infection of the brain; **sepsis**, which affects the blood; and pneumonia. Stroke is another dangerous risk. A stroke interrupts the flow of the blood to the brain, which kills brain cells and can cause loss of brain functions or death.

Staying Healthy

. . . .

Medical experts agree that one of the best ways for people with sickle cell disease to stay healthy is to avoid situations that may lead to pain crises.

Problem or Situation	How to Avoid It
Dehydration: exercise and kidney damage can cause loss of body fluids.	Drink plenty of fluids—six to ten 8-ounce glasses of water per day.
Exhaustion: when the body becomes over-tired, a chemical imbalance called lactic acidosis occurs.	While playing or exercising, take a fifteen to twenty-minute break for every hour of exercise.
Low oxygen levels	Avoid flying in small planes that are not fully pressurized with oxygen. Do not hike at high altitudes.
Temperature: both heat and cold can disturb blood flow.	When overheated, rest in the shade or in an air-conditioned room. When cold, seek a heat source and bundle up. Avoid getting too warm or too cold. When swimming in cold water, take breaks to towel dry and warm up. Do not use hot tubs. Wear warm-up clothes before exercising. Remove the clothes once the body heats up. Dress in layers, which can be removed or added according to temperature changes.

Infections: sickle cell disease weakens the immune system. Infections increase pain.	Get a flu shot to help prevent influenza and practice good hygiene, such as frequent hand washing. Young children (up to age six) should take daily doses of penicillin.
Stress: anxiety can often trigger a pain crisis.	Practice stress-reducing techniques and quiet activities such as taking warm baths, practicing yoga, acupuncture, resting, reading, and talking on the telephone. Get regular massages.
Small size or low weight: people with sickle cell disease are often smaller than their peers.	Generally, children with sickle cell anemia should consume about 20 percent more calories than those who do not have the disease. Whole milk, peanut butter, smoothies, milk shakes, and other high-calorie, nutritious foods help keep the body strong and energized.
Obesity: too much weight can put undue stress on hip and knee joints.	Follow a healthy diet and seek medical care from a nutritionist or dietician who can help design a personalized diet.

Meditation and yoga can help relieve some of the pain from sickle cell disease.

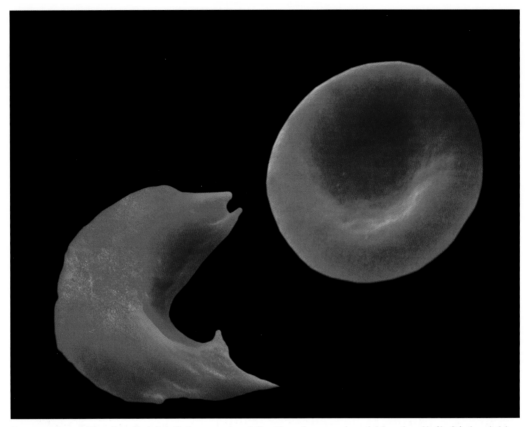

A normal red blood cell (right) is round, while the abnormal red blood cell (left) is sickle shaped.

Severe pain is another symptom of sickle cell disease. Pain occurs when the sickle cells block blood flow to an area of the body for an extended time. Without blood, the tissues die. This is a very painful experience called an **infarction,** or pain crisis. Some people might have only one brief crisis in a year, while others may experience more than a dozen crises that last for days or even weeks. Many pain crises occur in the hands, feet, abdomen, back, or chest. Certain activities and environments can trigger them. Triggers include lack of oxygen (at high altitude or in an airplane), exposure to hot or cold temperatures, dehydration, illness, fever, stress, or infection.

Two additional types of sickle cell disease are **sickle-hemoglobin C disease** and **sickle-beta thalassemia**. Like sickle cell anemia, these diseases are inherited. With just a single abnormal gene, a person can have either hemoglobin C trait or thalassemia trait. People with an abnormal hemoglobin gene trait rarely experience serious pain or illness, but they should avoid triggers such as strenuous exercise and dehydration. People with two abnormal genes have symptoms very similar to those of sickle cell anemia. People with hemoglobin C or thalassemia generally have ancestors who are from Africa, Asia, or Mediterranean countries. It is possible for people to inherit a combination of sickle-hemoglobin C disease, sickle-beta thalassemia, and sickle cell anemia.

3

THE HISTORY OF SICKLE CELL DISEASE

The Ga tribe of Ghana observed a disease that they called *chwechweechwe*. The Fante people called it *nwiiwii*. Other people in West Africa called it the body-chewing disease, or the disease of babies who come and go. Each culture was referring to sickle cell disease, which affects people from subtropical Africa more commonly than elsewhere in the world. In some African tribes, more than 40 percent of the population carries the sickle cell gene.

Because sickle cell disease resembles many other tropical diseases, it took a long time for people to recognize it as a unique condition. Africans began to study sickle cell disease in the 1870s. In the United States, the first mention of the disease was in a medical paper called "Case of Absence of the

Spleen," written in 1846. According to the report, a doctor was studying a corpse when he saw that the body had suffered "unfortunate" symptoms and was missing a spleen.

In 1904, a man named Walter Clement Noel moved to Chicago from the West Indies to study dentistry. He was often ill, and during one of his hospital visits, a young doctor named Ernest Irons took a sample of Noel's blood. Irons was surprised to see that Noel's blood had strange, "pear-shaped" red blood cells. Irons reported this to another doctor, James Herrick, who took care of Noel for two years before Noel returned home to Grenada. Herrick wrote that his patient had episodes of yellow eyes, shortness of breath, anemia, and rapid heart-beat. In 1907, not long after leaving Chicago, Noel died of pneumonia at the age of thirty-two.

A few years later, a woman named Ellen Anthony entered a Virginia hospital with a severe pain crisis. Her doctors real-ized that Anthony had been in the hospital many times previ-ously. When they drew her blood, they saw that her red blood cells were oddly shaped. One doctor recalled Herrick's report and determined that Anthony had the same symptoms as Noel.

Reports in medical studies in 1927 and 1940 note that sick-le cells carry less oxygen than normal red blood cells. Irving Sherman, a student at the Johns Hopkins School of Medicine, believed that the lack of oxygen was responsible for changing the shape of the red blood cells.

Sickle Cell Trait and Malaria

. . . .

Malaria is a serious, often fatal disease found in the tropics. The disease is transmitted by a mosquito from the genus *Anopheles*. Only female mosquitoes carry the disease. For many years, researchers have believed that sickle cell disease may have developed as a way for the body to resist malaria.

After an infected female Anopheles mosquito bites a person, the malaria parasites enter the host's red blood cells and begin to grow. But sickle cells die so quickly that the malaria parasites cannot spread. Researchers have found that only young people with sickle cell trait are able to fight off a malaria infection. Studies also show that people of African descent who have lived in malaria-free areas for long periods of time have fewer cases of sickle cell trait in their families than people living in Africa, where malaria is common.

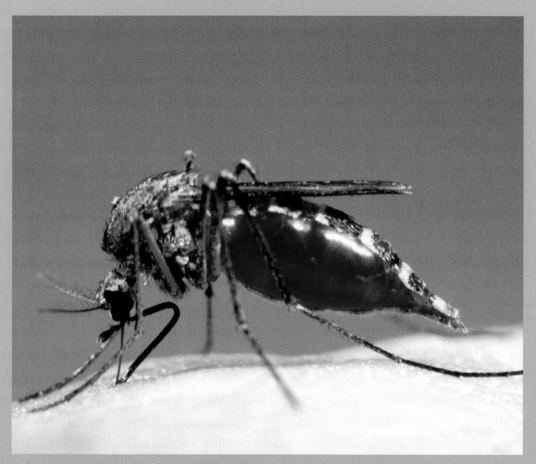

Malaria is transmitted by female mosquitoes.

In the 1940s, Linus Pauling of the California Institute of Technology, a future Nobel Prize–winning chemist, was studying molecules in the blood. Using a test called **electrophoresis**, he sent electric currents through red blood cells. By the way the molecules behaved, Pauling recognized that the hemoglobin molecules in red blood cells produce abnormal proteins.

In 1956, an English chemist named Vernon Ingram developed a method that proved that sickle cell anemia is an

Linus Pauling was a Nobel Prize-winning chemist who helped advance studies of sickle cell anemia.

inherited disease caused by a single amino acid (a building block of protein) in an abnormal hemoglobin molecule. In 1984, doctors performed a bone marrow transplant to treat a young girl with leukemia. The girl also had sickle cell anemia, and the procedure cured both diseases.

NEW TREATMENTS AND ADVANCES

Treatments for sickle cell disease have come a long way since the disease was discovered. Today, people with sickle cell disease can expect to live much longer and feel healthier than others did in the past. Health care professionals encourage people with sickle cell disease to follow healthy diets and to exercise moderately on a regular basis. Scientists are finding new medicines that reduce pain. Doctors are using new techniques and therapies, as well as performing surgery, to fight the disease. In addition, genetic researchers are investigating ways to correct the abnormal sickle cell gene.

The risk of stroke is a serious problem for people with sickle cell disease. A stroke occurs when the brain does not receive enough oxygen. Brain cells die, and there is no way to replace them. A stroke can cause a person to lose the ability to speak, to walk, or to understand normally. It can also cause death. Children with sickle cell anemia are more likely to suffer a stroke than adults who have the disease. Doctors fend off this danger with drugs that help red blood cells hold on to more oxygen. Researchers have also developed medications that replace some of the abnormal hemoglobin molecules with molecules of fetal hemoglobin. Fetal hemoglobin produces fewer sickle cells than sickle cell hemoglobin. Sometimes this medication is very helpful. Though it does not cure the disease, it often improves health and reduces pain.

Blood transfusions are another helpful treatment. Doctors transfer healthy blood from one person to another. The new, healthy blood replaces blood that has been trapped in the spleen. It may lower the risk of stroke. A blood transfusion also replenishes the body's red blood cell supply. The main risk of a blood transfusion is that too much iron can build up in the body. People who have frequent blood transfusions are tested for iron overload.

Children with sickle cell anemia are much more likely than adults to suffer serious illnesses such as meningitis and pneumonia. Because children sometimes have trouble fighting germs, infections can become serious very quickly. Many doctors prescribe **prophylactic** antibiotics, such as penicillin, for a child to take every day until age six or seven. Prophylactic treatments are small doses of antibiotics that are taken every day to help ward off germs until stronger medication is needed. Penicillin does not kill the germs, but it helps the body fight them off until stronger medications are required.

Scientists who study genes may hold the best hope for

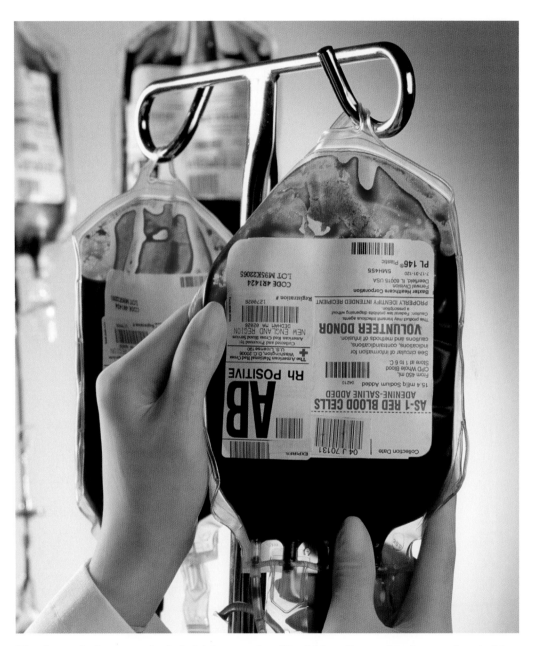

Blood transfusions may be helpful for people with sickle cell anemia who may be at risk for a stroke.

Famous People with Sickle Cell Anemia

....

- Miles Davis, jazz musician
- Paul Williams, singer
- T-Boz Watkins, musician
- Georgeanna Tillman, singer

T-Boz Watkins (right) appears onstage with fellow singer Rozonda "Chilli" Thomas. Watkins suffers from sickle cell anemia.

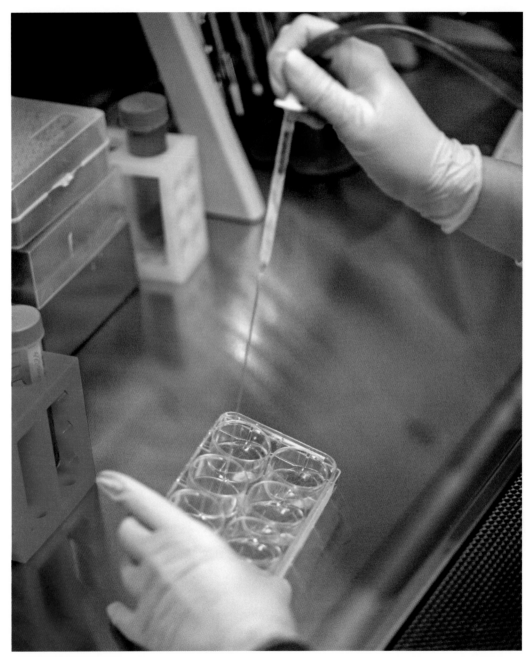

A laboratory worker prepares stem cells for testing.

control and cure of sickle cell disease. Some scientists research ways to change or replace the abnormal genes in hemoglobin with less harmful ones. Geneticists can also run tests on a woman to see if her unborn child has sickle cell anemia. This does not stop the disease from happening, but it allows parents and doctors to begin treatments early in a child's life.

Researchers are also developing treatments by using stem cells. Stem cells are immature cells found in babies as well as in adult's bone marrow. Their daughter cells can grow into any type of cell in the human body. Researchers have experimented with removing sickle cells, treating them with stem cells, and returning the red blood cells to the body. The new, normal red blood cells would help reduce pain and other symptoms.

For several years, doctors have performed bone marrow transplants on patients with sickle cell disease. This complicated operation requires finding another person who has genes and body tissue that are very similar to the patient's. The surgeon injects normal bone marrow into the patient in the hope that the new bone marrow will produce normal red blood cells. The operation has serious risks, however, and it is difficult to find a person who is a close genetic match. Doctors, researchers, and therapists continue to search for new ways to treat sickle cell disease. Many believe that gene therapy holds many answers—and possibly a cure—in the near future.

4

LIVING WITH SICKLE CELL ANEMIA

Sickle cell disease affects people and their families in a variety of ways. Sometimes the disease is painful and can disrupt school and family life. For others, the disease is moderate or mild. Patients, their families, and their medical care providers should create a personal plan for treatments and therapies, as well as daily activities.

HOW IS SICKLE CELL DISEASE DIAGNOSED?

It is very important to diagnose sickle cell disease early. The sooner the disease is discovered, the sooner treatment can begin. In the United States, doctors take a blood sample from every newborn baby. Called newborn screening, this blood test alerts doctors to any potential health problems. Most states require that newborn screening include a test for sickle cell

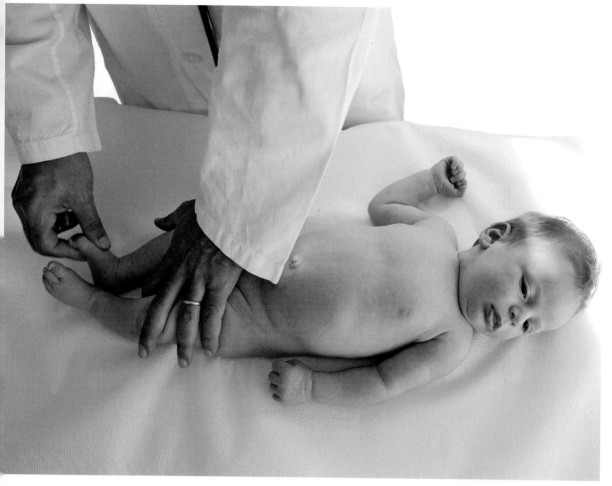

Blood is taken from newborns in order to detect certain diseases.

disease. This test can show whether the baby may have sickle cell anemia, sickle cell trait, sickle-beta thalassemia, or sickle-hemoglobin C. The newborn test is much like Linus Pauling's electrophoresis test. It is not, however, a final test for sickle cell disease. Babies carry HbF (fetal hemoglobin) in their blood for at least six months after birth, so a diagnosis cannot be complete until after that point. If the newborn screening test suggests that the baby may have a sickle cell condition, it is extremely important for the baby to be retested in six months.

A doctor who specializes in diseases of the blood is called a **hematologist.** Hematologists have several methods to test for sickle cell disease. A complete blood count shows the doctor how many red blood cells are present and how much hemoglobin is in them. A technician performs a blood smear and then studies the thin layer of blood on the glass side and views the number of blood cells. The technician can also detect whether any of the red blood cells are sickle shaped. Another test is called an HbS solubility test. The technician introduces a chemical that removes oxygen from the blood sample. If there are any HbS cells present, the reduced oxygen level will cause the HbS red blood cells to become sickle shaped. A final test is a genetic analysis. Doctors take a family history and look for sickle cell trait in other family members. Then doctors take a genetic sample to search for the sickle cell gene. Once the disease is confirmed, treatments should begin right away.

SYMPTOMS AND TREATMENTS

There are several symptoms of sickle cell disease, and there are several ways to treat or to prevent them. The most common

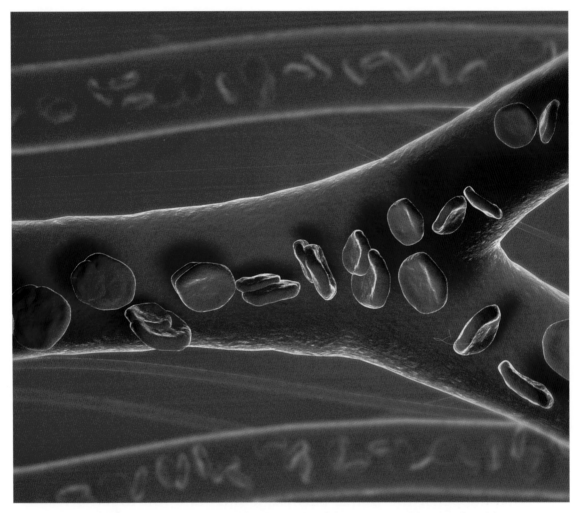

Normally, capillaries move through the blood vessels without any trouble. People with sickle cell anemia may have trouble with the blood vessels in their hands and feet becoming blocked.

symptom is pain, which is often very sharp and sudden. Pain can result from low oxygen, dehydration, infection, extreme heat or cold, too much exercise, or stress. People with sickle cell disease can treat mild pain with over-the-counter pain relievers such as acetaminophen or aspirin. Medicines such as ibuprofen or naproxen sodium may also help, but it is important to use only medicines that are approved by a doctor. Severe pain episodes often require strong pain medications, such as morphine, in a hospital setting. Many adults with severe pain take a drug called **hydroxyurea**, which reduces the number and strength of pain crises by increasing levels of fetal hemoglobin in the blood.

People who have severe sickle cell disease must be even more cautious about their condition. Some serious symptoms affect the extremities, such as hands and feet. Hand-foot syndrome is a condition where the blood vessels in the hands and feet become blocked, and this causes swelling and pain. Ulcers, which are open sores that do not heal, can appear on the lower legs, more often in males than in females. The blood supply that feeds the ends of bones in the shoulders and hip can become constricted, which causes the bone cells to die. When this happens, the bones become jagged and rub together. The joints hurt with every movement and can limit everyday activities. Surgeons can perform joint replacement surgery to remove the damaged joint and to replace it with an artificial joint. Most patients who have the surgery feel tremendous relief.

Sickle cell disease can damage a person's organs, too. Lack of oxygen can damage the retina of the eye. The vessels in the

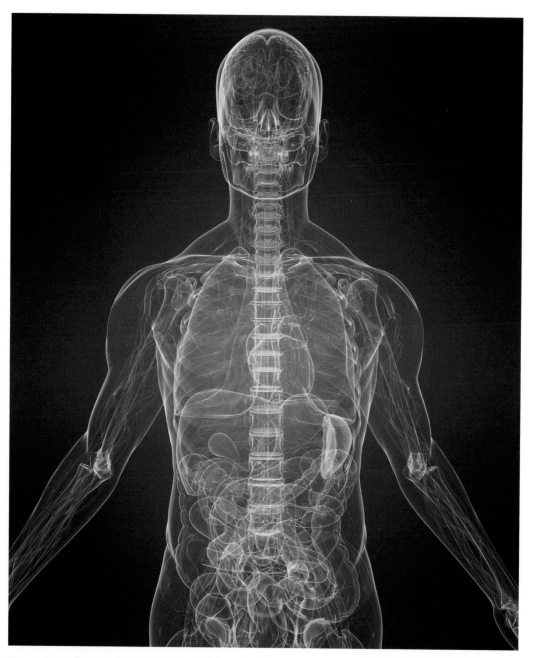

The spleen (highlighted above), which helps fight infections, becomes enlarged when sickle cells block the flow of blood.

lungs can become clogged, and this prevents the exchange of oxygen to the red blood cells. When the heart has a difficult time pumping blood through the lungs, the blood pressure increases and the patient experiences chest pain and shortness of breath. Blood vessels leading to the brain can also become blocked, which leads to a stroke. One type of stroke cuts off blood flow to the brain. The other type of stroke happens when a blood vessel bursts in the brain. Each type of stroke kills brain cells and can cause learning problems and physical disabilities.

Sickle cell disease often damages the spleen as well. The role of the spleen is to filter germs from the blood and to rid the body of abnormal red blood cells. The spleen can become clogged with dead sickle cells and cease to function properly. This results in pain and an inability to fight infections.

Infections are another source of serious concern to people with sickle cell disease. The disease affects the body's immune system and interferes with its ability to fight germs. Common germs can lead to pneumonia, meningitis, influenza, or hepatitis. In young children with severe sickle cell disease, these infections can be fatal.

Sickle cell disease has no definite cure, but today's treatments and therapies offer much promise. To achieve as enjoyable and pain-free a life as possible, people with sickle cell disease and their families need to take very active roles in

People with sickle cell anemia will have to visit the doctor more often than healthy people, but the doctors can help treat the disease.

managing their health. Patients should visit their doctors every two to six months. At a visit, a doctor will do a blood count and examine the patient's eyes, lungs, gall bladder, heart, spleen, and kidneys. Some doctors use an **ultrasonograph** to check for the possibility of a stroke. An ultrasonograph is a medical device that uses high-frequency sound waves (called ultrasound) to take a picture of the interior of the body. If the doctor is concerned about an increased risk of stroke—or if a stroke has occurred—he or she will likely recommend a blood transfusion. A blood transfusion is a common, safe method of transferring healthy blood from one person into the blood vessels of another person. For a person with sickle cell anemia, the oxygen-rich blood from the transfusion restores cells that have become injured or weak due to lack of oxygen. Transfusions also help relieve pain and prevent damage to many parts of the body. People with frequent or severe pain crises are likely to receive frequent blood transfusions.

People with life-threatening sickle cell disease can opt for a bone marrow transplant. Surgeons extract healthy bone marrow from a person who is a close blood type and tissue match. The person receiving the transplant must undergo chemotherapy and radiation in order to kill his or her own bone marrow. Then surgeons introduce the healthy marrow into the patient's bones with the hope that the new marrow will produce healthy red blood cells. This is a risky procedure, however. Radiation and chemotherapy are painful and very exhausting. A person already weakened by sickle cell disease often has difficulty enduring the treatments. There is a risk of infection afterward, as well as a risk that the patient's body will reject the new bone marrow. Doctors have been trying to avoid these complications by attempting to transplant only stem cells found in the marrow. Because the daughter cells of stem cells can

Pain Diary

· · · · · · · · · · · · · · · ·

People with sickle cell disease can help their caregivers determine the best treatment by keeping a pain diary. To be useful, a pain diary should include the following information:

- the location(s) of the pain
- descriptions of all symptoms that accompany pain, such as fever, cough, swelling, stomachache, or dizziness
- descriptions of the pain (for example, burning, throbbing, sharp, or dull)
- what helps reduce the pain
- what makes the pain worse
- how long the pain lasts
- how often pain crises occur
- possible triggers of pain crises
- a measure of the pain on a scale from one to ten (one is mild, and ten is unbearable)

mature into any type of cell, they can develop into healthy blood cells within the marrow.

MANAGING SICKLE CELL ANEMIA

Doctors and specialists encourage people with sickle cell disease to do all they can to manage pain and to control their symptoms. It is important for them to eat healthy foods such as fresh fruits and vegetables, whole grains, healthful fats (such as canola or olive oil), fish, and poultry. People should avoid eating too much red meat, fast food, snack foods, soda, and sweets. Many doctors recommend taking vitamin B9, also called folic acid, which helps the body produce red blood cells. People with sickle cell disease also need to balance their amount of exercise and activity. They need to keep their muscles strong and healthy while not overdoing exercise and taxing the body's resources.

Besides taking medicine, there are other ways to manage pain that comes from sickle cell disease. A heating pad, hot water bottle, hot bath, massage, or bed rest often help. Many people see a physical therapist, who uses special exercises and equipment to help people improve their flexibility and ease of movement. Physical therapists gently move affected parts of the body to help strengthen and stretch muscles and joints, and this often relieves pain.

Sometimes pain can cause people to become depressed or discouraged. People with sickle cell disease may benefit from

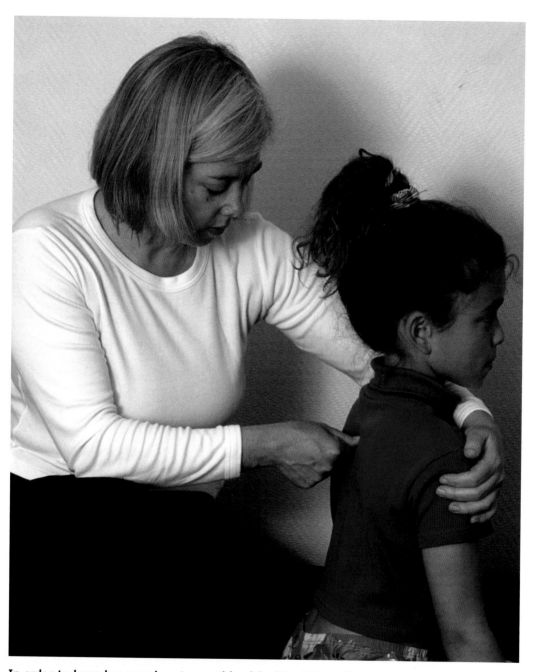

In order to keep her muscles strong, this girl with sickle cell anemia receives acupressure from a licensed therapist.

seeing a counselor, social worker, psychiatrist, or psychologist. These mental health care providers can show people how to relax and to practice strategies for ignoring pain and refocusing on more positive experiences.

Sometimes a "mind over matter" approach can relieve mild to moderate pain. Staying busy helps. Activities such as reading, watching movies, playing video games, or talking to friends on the telephone can take the mind off of pain. Physical exercise can also be helpful, though it is very important not to overexert the body. Physical activities such as swimming in warm water or walking can keep the body fit and healthy. Before becoming overtired or overheated, people with sickle cell disease need to take a break and rest. Many students are able to participate in physical education classes or school sports, but not without a doctor's approval.

Modern advances in medicine have given people with sickle cell disease many new treatment options and better ways of coping with the disease and its symptoms. Steps to maintaining a high quality of life are good health care, exercise, eating right, getting enough rest and fluids, avoiding situations that can cause pain crises, and knowing how to manage pain when it does occur. Family and friends can offer support every day, and it is important to let them know when they can provide help or comfort. Being open and honest with doctors about pain and other symptoms will help assure the best medical treatment. It is also important to educate teachers, classmates, coworkers, teammates, and coaches about sickle cell disease so that they will understand how to help when necessary.

Researchers around the world are hoping to find a cure for sickle cell disease. Many believe genetic research will be key. Meanwhile, more people with sickle cell disease are living longer and healthier lives than ever before.

GLOSSARY

alpha-globulin—A protein molecule found in plasma.

anemia—A deficiency of red blood cells.

antibiotic—A medication that fights bacterial infections.

beta-globulin—A protein found in plasma.

blood transfusions—Transfers of one person's healthy blood into another person's body.

capillaries—Small blood vessels that blood passes through as blood cells are nourished and cleared of waste.

contagious—Able to be spread from person to person.

daughter cells—A cell formed by the division of another cell.

dehydrated—Lacking necessary bodily fluids.

electrophoresis—A test used to identify the presence of abnormal proteins in hemoglobin.

erythrocyte—Another name for a red blood cell.

gamma-globulin—A protein found in hemoglobin.

gene—Substances that pass along characteristics from parent to child.

hematologist—A doctor who specializes in diseases of the blood.

hemoglobin—A protein found that binds to oxygen in red blood cells.

hydroxyurea—A medicine that helps reduce the strength and frequency of pain crises.

inherited—To have received from an ancestor.

infarction—The death of human tissue due to a lack of blood supply.

jaundice—A yellow tint to eyes and skin caused by the rapid breakdown of red blood cells in the liver.

meningitis—A serious infection that can occur in the brain and spinal fluid.

pain crisis—An episode of pain resulting from sickle cell anemia.

penicillin—A medicine that fights bacterial infections.

pneumonia—A serious infection of the lungs.

prophylactic antibiotic—A small dose of antibiotic taken daily to help the body fend off infections.

red blood cell (RBC)—One of the cells of the blood which carry oxygen to cells and tissues.

sepsis—A serious bacterial infection of the blood.

sickle cell disease—An inherited disease in which some red blood cells are C shaped and do not easily pass through blood vessels.

sickle cell trait—A genetic condition in which a person carries one abnormal sickle cell gene but does not develop the disease.

sickle-beta thalassemia—A type of sickle cell disease.

sickle-hemoglobin C disease—A type of sickle cell disease.

stem cells—Immature cells that can mature into any type of cell.

ultrasonograph—A medical device that uses ultrasound waves to take an image of the body.

venules—Small blood vessels.

FIND OUT MORE

Organizations

American Sickle Cell Anemia Association

10300 Carnegie Avenue

Cleveland, Ohio 44106

216-229-8600

www.ascaa.org

Sickle Cell Disease Association of America, Inc.

231 East Baltimore Street, Suite 800

Baltimore, Maryland 21202

800-421-8453

www.sicklecelldisease.org

The Sickle Cell Information Center

Grady Memorial Hospital

80 Jesse Hill Jr Drive, SE

Atlanta, Georgia 30303

404-616-3572

www.scinfo.org

Websites

KidsHealth: Do You Know About Sickle Cell Anemia?
http://kidshealth.org/kid/health_problems/blood/sickle_cell.html

National Heart Lung and Blood Institute
www.nhlbi.nih.gov/health/dci/Diseases/Sca/SCA_WhatIs.html

Sickle Cell Kids
www.sicklecellkids.org

Sickle Cell Society
www.sicklecellsociety.org

Books and Videos

Cosby, Bill. *To All My Friends on Shore*. (DVD). Digiview Productions, 2004.

Jones, Phill. *Sickle Cell Disease*. New York: Chelsea House Publishers, 2008.

Peterson, Judy Monroe. *Sickle Cell Anemia*. New York: Rosen Publishing, 2008.

Silverstein, Alvin, et al. *The Sickle Cell Anemia Update*. Berkeley Heights, NJ: Enslow Publishers, 2006.

INDEX

ABOUT THE AUTHOR

Ruth Bjorklund lives on Bainbridge Island, a ferry ride away from Seattle, Washington, with her husband, two children, and five pets. She has written several books about health issues.